Clint Faraday
Book thirty five
A Hit that Missed

Clint's nutty musician/botanist/author friend, Dave, discovers a new species of *Anthurium*. He is busy and will register it later. Some important people in the formal classification process come to Bocas Town because of the find.

Somebody then tries to kill Dave. Could it be because of the find?

Then a woman involved in the process is killed. That's going too far!

Contents

About the author

CD Moulton has traveled extensively over much of the world both in the music business, where he was a rock guitarist, songwriter and arranger and in an import/export business. He has been everything from a bar owner to auto salvage (junkyard) manager, longshoreman to high steel worker, orchid grower to landscaper, tropical fish farmer to commercial fisherman. He started writing books in 1983 and has published more than 350 books as of January 1, 2023. His most popular books to date are about research with orchids, though much of his science fiction and fantasy work has proven popular. He wrote the CD Grimes, PI series, and the Det. Nick Storie series, Clint Faraday series, and many other works.

He now resides in Gualaca, Chiriqui, Panamá, where he writes books, plays music with friends, does research with orchids and medicinal plants. He has lately become involved in fighting for the rights of the indigenous people, who are among his closest friends, and in fighting the extreme corruption in the courts and police in Panamá.

He offers the free e-book, *Fading Paradise*, that explains what he has been through because of the corruption.

CD is the discoverer of the Chadam Protocol for curing cancer.

Facebook page Ambrosia peruviana for cancer.

Clint Faraday
A Hit that Missed

Something Old, Something New

Clint Faraday, retired PI from Florida, arrived with his beautiful wife and young son in Bocas Town, Isla Colón, Bocas del Toro, Panamá, where he was greeted by his attractive next door neighbor, Judi Lum, and his nutty botanist friend, Dave. He had just come from Cusapín, on the Comarca Ngobe Bugle. He was raising his son in the Indio tradition. He brought his boat to his deck to find the two close friends there.

Judi helped him with his cases when he was in Bocas Town. She was a genius at getting information. She was attractive and smart, but could act the airhead to perfection. They unloaded the boat and stowed their things. They would stay in Bocas Town for about two months, then would go to Quebrada Tula, on the comarca inland, then to Cusapín on the coast, then back again to Bocas Town or for a shorter stay in the David area.

"How are things around here?" Tyna, his wife, asked.

"Same old same old," Judi answered. "Not very much changes here except prices. They're getting ridiculous. We used to go to Almirante once a month for canned goods and such and to David twice a year for clothes and that kind of thing. Now we go to Almirante at least every week. The residents don't buy on the island much. It's all for the tourist trade. We used to go to the better restaurants, but they've gotten so high we don't anymore. The season's almost over and they'll drop their prices. We've pretty much agreed to not trade with them anyhow.

"I was talking to Yveth at the market. She said the cost of bringing things to the island was why the prices went up. I told her the price of beer went up exactly four cents. It costs the same to buy it here as Almirante. Beer's sixty five cents in Almirante and a dollar and a half here. She said one of them raised their price, so they all had to. It doesn't get through to her that keeping the price down would mean they got all the business. Tuna delivery didn't go up eighty cents a can, it went up a quarter of a cent a can. We resent most that they think we're stupid enough to fall for that line!"

"Beer went up in David, too," Clint said. "From sixty to sixty five."

"They don't have so many stupid gringos who'll pay whatever and claim it's still a hell of a lot cheaper than the states or Costa Rica," Dave said. "I'll go to my place in David tomorrow. I found a few new things in the mountains that got my interest. The plant is just different enough that it could be a new variety of *Scaphyglottis*. There was an *Anthurium* I want to watch. It's a little different, but those are pretty well classified. Finding a new one would make a hell of a splash and a big name for someone if it's showy enough. That bromeliad I took pictures of has the experts arguing. I'm certainly no expert.

"Anyhow! We can spend some time together catching up tonight. Selma's here now. She'll go back to Las Tablas next week. Ben and Earl are in the states, then to England, then back here. Tom is moving to Ecuador. Maybe he'll find someone there who'll put up with his shit."

They chatted awhile, then Clint and Tyna took Nito, their son, and went into town to talk with the people they knew. It was pleasant, but they didn't go to the regular bars or restaurants.

Things rocked along tranquilly for a week and a half, then Dave came back with a lot of pictures of the *Anthurium* he'd found. It looked like an entirely new species. He was going to send the pictures to the major places to see if it had been identified anywhere before. Missouri Botanical Gardens, Kew and others.

Foreigners Arrive

It wasn't thirty six hours before a man arrived from England. As soon as he saw the pictures he jumped on a flight and got there fast! This one had everything! A number of them had very nice plants and some had very showy flowers, greens, reds, orange, yellow. This one was purple, very rare, and was large and showy. In addition, the plant was a beauty, in itself! He just *had* to see the plant *in situ*!

Dave refused. He said to show anyone where it was would more likely mean it would be extinct in its natural habitat in a month or less. Dr. Collin Edward Blakely was not going to know where that plant was!

"There is only the one? Then it's a hybrid, more than likely. I can find the parents and we can grow as many as we want from seed!"

"There are pictures of nine different plants here. They're found just a little distance apart. It's not a hybrid. It's an extremely localized species," Dave replied.

"You'll have to describe the exact location with a GPS locator, so this is silly! You can't register it as something found in Chiriqui, Panamá, anymore.

Those days are gone forever."

"Then I won't register it. Next argument. I'm not telling anyone where it's found. I've crossed three of them. I can grow the seeds and register it from that."

Blakely was somewhat effeminate and looked like he would throw a screaming fit. His voice had already gotten higher. Dave looked over to where Clint and Judi were sitting. They were in the Golden Grill. People were turning to look at Blakely and Dave. Blakely noticed and abruptly caught himself.

"You have to realize how important this is to science," he said. "This species exhibits several things that are rare in *Anthurium*. The color and size isn't all!"

They argued more quietly. Clint could have told Dr. Blakely that arguing with Dave where the preservation of a species was concerned was like arguing with a brick wall.

Clint had an idea. He went over to them and asked, "Dave, didn't you say you found them in the comarca?"

Dave saw what he was doing. "I might have. It might or might not be true. Why?"

"Because we can see that no one goes onto the comarca after them."

"That's right! I had to get Basilio and Silvio to

give *me* permission!

"I still won't say. This type will find a way to sneak in and steal them. I never could understand it. I was in Honduras in the fifties, when they were having the orchid wars. They would literally kill each other to be able to say they'd found a new commercial variety. This would damned well be commercial! I think. There're a few things that could mean it will never be, but they'd wipe them out, anyhow.

"Blakely, I'll raise the seeds and give them to the world, but I won't take you or anyone else, up to and including God, to them *in situ*. It's all too possible I can't even do that. They're growing in rather specialized conditions. I will note that every one I've found is at a specific altitude. That could be for a lot of reasons, one of which is that they won't grow anywhere else. It's also wet in a specialized way. The altitude thing alone would limit them to a very few places. The season thing would tend to limit their distribution even more. I don't know the critical elevation differences. If they won't survive below sixteen hundred meters or above sixteen hundred fifty meters and have to be on a rotting hardwood log above a stream with sixty percent shade in cloud forest moisture part of the year and drier part of the year, you've lost ninety nine percent of the places they can survive.

If the temperature variation over the year is limited to days between sixty five and seventy and nights to between fifty five and sixty three, you can only grow them where they're found. Nowhere else. That could be the restrictions that kept them from being all over the mountains.

"What if they're like *Otoglossum chirigense*? What if the places they can survive are limited to almost straight up and down in a high wind area in full sun at the base of the rain forest? Then where are you?"

"Getting your name on a new species like this one is the most ... I mean, your name would live forever! Look at Cattley!"

"This ain't no genus with nearly the potential of *Cattleya*!" Dave fired back. "Get a grip!"

Blakely caught himself again. He suggested they would discuss it later, when they were both in more reasonable moods. They really should be talking about preserving the species, of course. He could see Dave's argument, but they would find a way to protect them. Dave said to find the way first, then they could discuss other issues.

The next day Susan Carole Knight came from Malaysia. She was interested in classifying the plant and was sure it wouldn't involve any great difficulty. She wanted first crack at some of the seeds. They would prove a very good market was still possible in tropicals.

Dave talked with her. Blakely was there for part of it and was steaming because she was getting a more positive response from Dave.

The next day seven more people came because of the find. Dave was so exasperated he couldn't even talk straight. When they came to him to talk about the *Anthurium* he'd walk away. It was the first time Clint ever saw him deliberately rude. They all wanted to have exclusive rights to name it. They'd name it after him, which he couldn't do himself if he was registering it. They seemed to think that was all he would ever want in life! The greatest discovery in *Anthurium* in more than a hundred years would carry his name!

"And they would have their name listed as the discoverer of the greatest discovery in *Anthurium* in a hundred years! I would just be some schnook they named it after. Kiss my royal rusty ass! I'm damned sorry I ever sent those pictures. I don't want it in my name. I don't want to be famous for something as stupid as that! You know I always name the orchids I find after friends. I could work any kind of deal with any number of people with the orchids to have my name on something like nine new species I've already found here. Instead, they're *Scaphyglottis basilioi* and *Epidendrum silvioanum* and *Sobralia estebaniae* and so forth. Damn!

"If I get to name this one, it's going to be *Anthurium clintonitoae*, after your kid."

He put up with it for two more days, then Clint got a call. He was in the mountains, he wouldn't say where. He wasn't coming back until that bunch were gone. Take care of his plants.

"And Clint, you have one of these *Anthurium*. It's that thing in the Stryofoam chest beside the swamp cooler under the dark chocolate-brown *Catasetum*. It should start to bloom soon. Please pinch off any buds until this mess is over!"

Clint walked out on his deck. The plant was there and there were two buds just beginning to show. He pinched them off and told Dave he'd done it. He would watch for more.

Another day passed. Dave called and said he thought someone had found him up there and was following him. He wasn't in the near area of the *Anthurium* and wouldn't go near them so long as any of that gaggle were in Panamá.

"Clint? Could you accidentally drop a hint that I found them in Calderas?"

"No. That would be too obvious. However, Judi could yak something about it that they'd believe."

Dave laughed. "That would be an act I'd like to see! She's a genius with it!"

That night Judi was talking to a couple of the foreigners who asked if Dave had found anything new and interesting near La Fortuna. She acted distracted and said that he found all those crazy things around Calderas the past few months. Everybody and his dog had looked for things in La Fortuna. If it was as big as a quarter, it had already been found. An hour later two of them had taken the water taxi to Almirante. They could get the David bus there and go to Calderas from David. They could spend a few wasted weeks looking over the probable locations where it wasn't.

Judi said she was going to drop a hint that Dave first mentioned the *Anthurium* when he got back from Darien, but he also went to Palenque and Porto Bello that trip, so she didn't have a clue – and did she remember to turn off the stew? Oh, crap! The last time it *ruined* her best pot!

Dave called the next afternoon and said someone had fired a gun close that had barely missed him. It would have been right through his ear if he hadn't jerked his head just then because of a deer fly. He was beside a big nispero. The shot hit the tree right there. He didn't know if it was deliberate. Clint told him to get out of there and go to his place in David. Better yet, to Cusapín. He knew damned well no one could get to him there.

Tyna asked what was wrong when Clint rang off.

"I think it wasn't a great idea to let those people think they could find the *Anthurium* in Calderas. They can go almost anywhere there and the area description, if true, would mean there were only sixty or seventy hectares where it could be. Now they think they can find it and he would only be a hindrance."

"But they're on their way to Calderas now."

"You know damned well it costs a couple of hundred bucks for a hit here."

"Would a hit man miss?"

"Not if he were professional. This was probably someone they found down around sixth street or in

Changuinola or somewhere. There wouldn't be a hit that missed with a professional. Maybe, if he jerked his head at the critical instant. We don't even know that. I'd have to see what the area's like. A professional might think he'd hit him and leave. An amateur would probably just keep on shooting."

He called Dave. "What was the area like?"

"What do you mean?"

"Were you where you could be seen?"

"Be seen? I don't ... oh. No. The shot was from across to a rock outcropping on a little hill or from a taller tree. Maybe a thousand feet away. Twelve hundred. Fifty or sixty meters higher. The path was an animal trail I was on. Thick foliage except passing that tree. It was damned steep to that side and only low ground scrub. I made damned sure I couldn't be seen from over there again."

Clint took that as meaning he was passing a tree on a narrow trail where only that one spot was visible to someone on a nearby hill that was a little higher than his position. Still no way to tell if it was a professional. Possibly. The shot was dead center at a thousand feet or more. An amateur good shot with a good scope might do it.

Clint thought. He called Dave again. "Were you coming or going?"

"What the hell does ... oh. Returning. I went in fifteen or twenty minutes before."

Clint thought more and shook his head. This one could be mean. It was a professional who found his target spot when Dave went in. Sniper training.

"So we don't know if it was a pro. Probably.

"Tyna, I'm going to David." She nodded. Dave was a friend. Clint wouldn't let this go.

Clint packed a few things, played with Nito a minute. He explained that a friend was in danger. He had to go. Nito, at just over one year of age, understood how his father was.

He went over to Judi's deck on the way out to explain what had happened. She'd keep her ears open. Several in the group of foreigners were of a psychology like Blakeley's. Obsessed with getting their name on the discovery. She already knew there was a lot of infighting among them.

"Markam and Schone and LeSeur in particular. There are people from seven or eight countries here now. Dr.s Schone and Markham went to Calderas. Edna Markham, Australia, and Liam LeSeur, Switzerland. Gustav Schone is German. There's a Pedro Castro from Brazil and a Gina Bianco from Italy. All are doctors of botanical science or like degrees.

"Why all this over a damned plant Dave found? What's worth killing for?"

"It's like the iris and orchid wars. A new big discovery in today's greedy world can mean you get umpty million dollars if you're exclusive. I think this bunch of pigs want their name on the discovery. It will mean eternal fame."

"Get real! Eternal fame?"

"Col. Cattley? Registered an orchid in eighteen something and half the hybrids collectors and florists in the world use depend on that orchid for form and size and so forth? You grew orchids in the states. How many *Cattleya* hybrids? What about the *Cattleya* types here?"

"Sheesh!"

He soon headed for Almirante and his car. He wouldn't let Dave know he was coming. Yet.

Clint checked into the Palacio Imperial. It was far enough from downtown to where he could select where he'd be seen. He called Dave and suggested he keep a very low profile. Dave said he was going to Cusapín with some friends from there who were in David to buy supplies. He'd get in touch when he was there.

Clint waited until just before dinner time to go into David. He had heard of a place around the corner from the Iris, Disfrutas, that served the best chichas in David. He went in to try it and decided on the guanabana/aguacate. It was as good as the place's reputation. Delicious!

Clint sat at a table by the front window. There was a gringo there who waved him to the seat. He said he was living in Puerto Armuelles at the moment, but was moving to David in a week or so. Clint said he was from Florida, as was Mike Taylor, his new acquaintance. He was living in Bocas Town at the moment, but spent equal time on the comarca at Quebrada Tula and equal time at Cusapín. Mike said he knew somebody who went to Cusapín and everywhere else. A botanist who studied orchids.

He was also a musician who had played with some big name bands in the late sixties and early seventies.

"Not Dave?" Clint asked.

"Yeah. You know him?"

"He's a friend. He has a place in Quiteño that's been stolen by some local crooks. He's trying to get it back, but the system here is so corrupt it's taken three years already while the fiscalía drags it on and on. He thinks someone's been paid to do that.

"He's found a new species of *Anthurium*. The registration people are driving him crazy – not that he isn't already.

"You're Mosaic Mike? He's mentioned you."

Mike laughed. "He stayed at my place in Punta Piedra a couple of times. I'll bet he does go nuts when those greedbags bug him. He'll probably go somewhere nobody will know and disappear for a month or so."

"That, I don't doubt! He's gotten himself into some kind of deep shit over this. We think one of them tried to have him killed."

"Are you sure it's one of them? He's had two attempts on him here from, he thinks, anyhow, the ones who have his land tied up. He's going to go public about that. It could be politicians. He doesn't let it worry him."

"He did? Why in hell doesn't he tell me these

things?!"

"He doesn't take them seriously. He wanders all over town half the night in some of the worst sections.

"Okay. So there aren't any really bad sections here. Not like Costa Rica and Colón and parts of Panamá City. He laughs at how much amateurs they are. He knew real mafia dons in California. It doesn't matter if it's an amateur or professional on the trigger. If they get you, you're just as dead.

"He says it doesn't matter how fast you can draw if you can't hit anything."

"This one seemed like a trained sniper, by the way it was done. Know of anyone like that here?"

"Nah. Only the shit-shovelers. Some dude who claims to have been a Navy SEAL. Can't speak English."

"You sure he wasn't?"

"He wasn't. It's like that Rick character who claimed to be with Interpol. If he was, the last thing he'd do is say so. It's bullshit!"

They chatted awhile. Clint had learned about the attempted hits and the political mess. Dave wasn't the type to mention them to his detective friend!

Mike was quite the character. Clint was sure he'd see him around more. He finally said he had to check up on a few things and headed for the Iris.

A woman in her early thirties was talking with

Peter, the owner of the bar. He introduced Clint to Dr. Edna Markham, from Australia. She was there doing some botanical research, looking for new species.

"Oh, yes. I saw you in Bocas. In front of the Bahia, I believe. There for that stupid mess about Dave's new *Anthurium*. Twenty of you trying to get the right to name it.

"Ain't gonna happen. He's already made very damned sure it'll be named *clintonito*, after my son.

"You here because he was in Calderas a lot?"

She took a few seconds to stabilize herself. "Uh, yes. Dr. LeSeur and I. We feel we have to search every area he might have been studying.

"You say he left instructions about naming it? Do they show where he found it?"

"What a strange thing to ask! You asked if he left it? What do you mean?"

"He left Bocas Town. He left instructions about naming the plant. What else could I mean?"

"Oh. I thought you were saying he left Panamá or that he died. No. He has that with him if he ever wrote it down. He might have left it with Silvio if he found it on the comarca this side. It would be with Basilio if it was on the Caribbean east part. I think the first time I heard anything about it was when he came back from Darien. I don't really remember. He's always finds new species, but mostly orchids of botanical interest.”

“He mentioned when ... but Darien is huge! A lot of it has never been explored!”

“That’s why he goes there. Judi would know more about that kind of thing. Judi Lum. She’s my neighbor in Bocas Town. She’s a close friend of all of us.”

“Yes. I’ve met her. She’s the one who said he talked about it when he came from Calderas.”

“I see.”

“She’s not reliable? I mean, she didn’t seem to ... I don’t know. She was talking about something and someone asked her if he told her where it was from. She said he’d talked about it ... not about it directly. More about strange things he’s found. The question was about that plant though.”

“If she wasn’t concentrating on that question she probably only heard part of it or something. You never know. She might have meant that one. Maybe.”

She sighed, and grinned. “Would you tend to say ‘Flighty?’ She might have been thinking about strange rocks?”

“Well, he did find some turquoise and amethyst there. And jade.”

“Well, it’s a lot easier than Darien. I’ll spend some time on it.”

Jessy called Clint. He nodded and went to her. She

said he was to have Dave call his lawyer. It was very important. He said he'd try to get a message to him. He looked around and didn't see anybody, so went out. Just as he approached the door to the stairs he heard Markham talking on her cellular, "... said he thought it was from Darien. Try to get that Lum woman to tell you something. He says that you have to make her concentrate or her answers might well be about something else ... I can't say ... He seemed to think it's not here ... Call me when you get anything."

He stepped back and went toward the door as if he were coming from the balcony. She smiled, and said, "Good night!" He went on out.

He stopped on the corner in front of Romero's and called Dave with the message to call his lawyer, then went back to the Palacio Imperial and worked with his computer awhile, then walked down to Coco on the Green for a beer and to chat, then went back to the hotel and sacked out.

In the morning he got a call from Judi. Schone and Bianco had cornered her at the China and grilled her a bit about Darien. She told them just about what she'd suggested.

He went across the street for a good typical breakfast. He was halfway through when he got another call. From Sergio Sanchez, head of the violent crimes police department on the Bocas del

Toro archipelago.

"Clint? You were looking into those people who came because of Dave's big discovery?"

"Yes. I'm here in David to see what I can find."

"Judi says someone tried to shoot him?"

"Yes. Why?"

"Because one of them got shot. Susan Knight. She was the one Judi said was working with him, not against him."

"Oh, shit! Where? How? When?"

"On the road near the airport. Directly through the side of her head, one inch above her left ear. Half an hour ago. She was going to meet the Panamá City flight."

"Close?"

"No. It was professional. The shot was heard coming from behind the hotel there. No one saw anyone around the area."

"So. We had one try that missed. This one made the target. Susan was the only one of that bunch who was willing to go along with Dave to help preserve the species. This takes it out of the other possibilities, I think."

"Other possibilities?"

"Dave is getting politics and publicity into his legal crap. The bunch he's after use hits to scare people into not testifying against them. It was a road to investigate when it was just Dave being shot at."

"You thought that was why Dave was shot at?"

"I'll tell you about it. I'll be back in Bocas as fast as I can get there. I have to assume this is a professional hit. Look at anyone who came there in the last week. It's too well-planned to be less than someone with experience. One – or some – of those plant people knows who to hire at a moment's ... now it doesn't add up anymore. They're a bunch of doctors of science. They're the college professor type."

"I see what you mean. I'll conduct a very close investigation of all of them and anyone else who came recently. There's a lot more to this than some plant."

"It could be about the plant, Sergio. That's what makes it so hard. Getting rights to that plant is getting a few fast millions of dollars, believe it or not."

"If you say so, I believe it. I don't have any knowledge of such things."

"I'll be there in about four hours. We'll get together and try to sort this out."

He rang off and got his maleta, then got in his car and headed for Almirante. Something was a long way off balance in this thing. Sergio was probably right about it not really being about the *Anthurium*. This might be an opportunity someone grabbed to take care of a problem that was around before the plant came up. A check of all their pasts could expose something else.

It was raining all the way from above Mali to Almirante, which slowed him a little. He still made it to the island in four hours.

"I investigated all of them in a surface way, but don't expect it to tell us much," Sergio said. "They're what they seem on the surface so far. A group of university professors in competition to name a plant and claim rights of discovery. Schone and Castro want the honor, apparently. Bianco wants to see the exact conditions where the plant is found in. A lot of things are found only in Panamá and Brasil and Costa Rica and Brasil. Dave found those things that are only found in Ecuador and Panamá.

"I would put Castro out of it. Schone, down on the list, but still on it. Bianco, down on the list. I'm going to concentrate on Blakely, LeSeur and Markham."

"I have another slant to look into. It's mostly just a gut feeling," Clint replied. "I'll go on to my place and check some things on the computer. I'll come back this afternoon to compare notes."

Clint went home to play with Nito until Judi came over. She had checked on people on the island who didn't fit in one way or another.

"Don't fit? What do you mean?" Tyna asked.

"Well, I figure a hit man wouldn't fit in with anything here. People are here for vacations or surfing or investment or whatever. You have the professors who don't fit except in their own little group, and they're in competition and don't get along with each other. The one who did fit, Susan Knight, was murdered. She was working with Dave, who they tried to kill.

"I asked myself, 'Who on this island fits with Blakely, and how?' You know how fast he got here. He didn't find out about it that fast through the registration board, like Susan did. He would have been at least a day later. Susan represented a conservation group who watch for these kinds of discoveries and react immediately.

"Do you see what I'm saying?"

"Who here fits in with that bunch?" Clint asked. "I've thought a little along those lines. I've been wondering whether someone thinks Dave told Susan something or whether Susan might have told Dave something."

"It won't be anywhere near where the plant is found," Judi said, positively.

"No. That's true."

"I don't understand?" Tyna said.

"If Dave told Susan where it is they would have followed her until they found it. They definitely wouldn't have killed the very one who could lead them to the prize," Clint explained. "Someone was very much afraid Dave would find or had found something in those mountains – and it will be in the area where he was shot at. Maybe they were afraid he told her about it. That would mean the plant doesn't have a damned thing to do with it. Someone here, as Judi suggested, would be behind it, if not the killer directly.

"The place he was shot at isn't that close to the comarca, is it?"

"Where was it?" Tyna asked. "As exactly as you can say."

"I'll have to ask Sergio," Clint said. He called.

"It was close to Jaramillo Amba. It wasn't really Calderas. Close, though."

Clint told Tyna. She nodded. She said that was a couple of kilometers from the comarca, no more. That part of the comarca is high. Not many people go there. She had a first cousin who moved to Jaramillo with her boyfriend, who she was going to marry when she had the baby. She took the phone and looked up a number. She chatted awhile in Ngobe. When she hung up she said there were some gringos who went through Jaramillo, some-times. They had a small finca on the river between the town and the comarca. They were heard talking about raising trout, but there wouldn't be people in the area to make the kind of place like the one near

Cerro Punta pay off. They could raise them for the retail market and probably do fairly well if they were big enough. It would be a better area to raise prawns.

"I think I want to see what they're really raising there," Clint said. "It ain't gonna be trout."

"I may have heard something about Jaramillo," Judi said. "I'm trying to remember who said ... it was about it being close to something.

"That place Harry Fairbanks has! He was the one who was talking about raising fish, but it was Tilapia, not trout! It was at the Grill, a year or more ago. Jim said it was probably too cold up there for Tilapia. Your good buddy, Tom (one of the few people Clint could not bring himself to tolerate), said to raise prawns."

"Fairbanks? That big guy living out toward The Bluffs? Goes to the states for six months, then here six months?"

"Yes. His wife was here for a couple of years, then said she couldn't stand living here and went back. He's had a couple of other women who lived with him six months. He brought them from Oregon or wherever," Judi answered.

Clint looked thoughtful, but didn't say anything. After awhile he said he'd better get to the station to see what Sergio had found.

Sergio reported that they were all your standard

university professor types. The name of the school and the things they'd published were like those TV show for a couple of years in the eighties. Same story, you changed the town and the people's names. He'd watched two on TV a week apart on different channels. He could quote the lines from the second. It was exactly like the first.

Clint nodded. "Even the same personality.

"Sergio, what do you know about a Harold James Fairbanks?"

"The big man out near The Bluffs?"

"Uh-huh."

"Not much. He doesn't mix much and spends half his time in David and Panamá City. Wife refuses to come here so he brings other women. Has a small Toyota truck here and a Chevrolet in Almirante. Here on inversionista residencia. He's a corporation. Has some kind of deal with that Goodman ass."

"Goodman ass?"

"Building a condominium or two. Gonna make a hundred million bucks a month. Can't talk about anything but his money. I thought it was laundering at first, but he's clean on that point."

"Get word out that I'm in Panamá City. I have to disappear for a few days."

"You might be anywhere but Panamá City."

Clint grinned. He thought for a few minutes on the

way back to his house. This might get hairy. Tyna and Nito were not going to be where some professional killer could get to them.

He went on to Judi's place first to chat. She agreed with him. She said she could use a bit of vacation time as a respite from her life, which was a constant vacation.

About an hour later Judi, Nito and Tyana took Clint to Almiramte, then took the boat on and out past Isla Popa to Cusapín. Both Judi and Tyna were experts with the boat. They would be safer in the comarca than anywhere else. If anyone there was asked if they were there they would be told Tyna had mentioned Quebrada Tula, where she had a house. She made the agreement with Basilio and several others. As she was leaving she stopped and said, "Quebrada Tula. There! You won't be lying. I mentioned Quebrada Tula several times."

Clint took his car from Almirante to David, stayed the night in David, then headed out toward Panamá City. He had an Indio friend who traded his Jeep four wheel drive for Clint's car for a few days. It would only be used in emergencies. Clint had to return the Jeep with a full tank of gas.

<u>*Martín Quinteros Rides Again*</u>

The very proper impeccable dark man left his borrowed Jeep at the farm and rented a fine horse to use while exploring the area. The big Mexican "Vicente Fernandez" hat seemed to fit him. He had a thin silver-headed black cane and Rolex wristwatch and a large diamond ring on one of his perfectly manicured fingers with a silver and turquoise holder for his white tie bandana. He spoke excellent Spanish in a quiet cultured voice. He rode casually to Jaramillo Amba and fluidly dismounted the fine Palomino. He went into the little restaurant and sat to order chicken and rice with frijoles and patacones and guanabana chicha and to chat a bit with the pretty woman running the place. He said he was from Madeira. He was looking at the smaller towns in the mountains. He liked the country life and would have a finca to raise fine horses, such as the one he had rented just before the puebla. He said he heard about Jaramillo Amba in a restaurant in Bocas Town. Some big gringo was talking about raising fish in a finca nearby.

"Morris Goodman and his friend. They come past here sometimes. Morris can only talk about money.

The big one he calls 'Harry' is alright, but he doesn't talk much."

"Ah, yes. The big pale man who is always with a woman not his wife."

"There was only one time he was with a woman here. She was very much like a bank teller. She was so formal! 'Buenos dias!' sounded false. You understand? Like she said it only because the boss said she must."

"Yes. So I've heard. They have a finca near the comarca."

"Yes. Only perhaps a hundred meters from the comarca. We Indigenas don't very much care for them, but they are not unwelcome. We do not understand their ways and they do not understand ours. We try to understand them, they do not try to understand us." Clint could hear the slight resentment in her tone.

"Yes. They seem the arrogant greedy kind of people. They do not care to hear that their greed is from an emptiness in their souls that cannot be filled with things. They will waste their entire lifetimes seeking what they are avoiding. It is quite sad. I pity such people. They cannot know contentment for more than a minute."

"But they are religious, I think. They should know of the salve for the soul from their church. Their church is greedy for things, we notice."

"I did not speak of the soul in the preachings of their churches. I am not religious, though my parents were very much the strict Catholics. I meant that thing inside us all that seeks the very contentment they can never know. It cannot and will not be found in things. It is found in knowing other people, not in competition with them. It is found in unity with others, not in separation from them for silly non-reasons. Contentment is found in sharing a song or a sunset, work and play."

"You think much like we Indigenos."

They chatted a bit longer. The food was very good. There was plenty of it. Several Indigeno workers came in for lunch and he chatted with them. He spoke their language perfectly, but they didn't know that. He was pleased when they said, in Guayme, that he seemed to be a very good man, not like so many who came from the cities. He could be called a friend. He thought like a friend and acted like a friend. He was interested in the truth, not in only acting like he was interested. He was obviously a proud and very wealthy man, but not an arrogant one.

He walked around the puebla for awhile, then mounted and rode on toward the comarca. He'd learned the road there ended at the Goodman finca gate without asking or seeming curious about the gringos.

The country was beautiful, but most of Panamá is. When he was close to the river he could see that there were a few houses along it where the natives seemed to be raising prawns. They were large and plentiful. They didn't take them to sell anywhere, but the gringos would sometimes buy them. They raised them for their own use. Clint, or Martín, stopped to chat with all he met. These were a very friendly and curious people.

There was a four-row barbed wire fence around the Goodman finca and signs that said, "Privado! No entrarse!" (Private! Do not enter!) He hadn't seen any such signs anywhere before he saw that. There were small signs that said "Privado," but it was for information to let people know it wasn't government land.

He rode around the fence line to the river and along the bank of the river. The river is public property. The water level was low, so he was on public property. He rode to the far side and back around to the road/path. He saw one place where there was a thin overgrown path where a person could cross the river by placing boards across the rocks that the river moved between, forming a cascada/rapid flow. It was only about two o'clock, so he rode to the spot and went a distance downstream, where the water was only a few inches deep with a pebbly flat crossing point, then back up to the path on the far side. He noted that the path was overgrown very recently. They probably came every month or so and cut a new path each time. The forest would take over in little time.

The path went into the comarca and led to a little lush valley with a narrow agua viviendo quebrada (living water creek. "Agua viviendo" means there's always a flow. It doesn't dry up in the drier season) running through it. There didn't seem to be anything else there. There was a tree that he'd seen in Florida a lot, but not in Panamá. Chinaberry. Most places it was called Neem. There were a few bananas, usually plantains in Chiriqui Province, though there were bananas everywhere at lower altitudes. A few pineapples. Mormónes. They seemed random, not planted. Like they just grew there. There were a lot of places like that in the mountains. There was a small apple tree. That was a little out of place, seeing there was an orange tree and a lemon tree. Everything that was normally found in such places, yet not in quite that mix.

He went to inspect some of the fruit trees and so forth. The leaves on the orange tree seemed just a small bit ... different. They were of a somewhat different texture than normal. The mormón, ditto. The mormón leaves had a slight lobing. That was also true of the orange and lemon.

He was about to taste them, then thought better of

it. This could be the type of thing caused by radiation. He'd found radium and uranium in ores near Puerto Armuelles.

Were they afraid Dave had found they had a lode of uranium or something? How would he know? He didn't carry a Geiger counter and his digital cameras wouldn't show radiation fogging.

The subtle differences in the plants. Dave was a botanist. He would see that immediately. He would know it could be the kind of thing radium or uranium ores could cause.

Wouldn't he?

He called Dave, but there was no signal there. He couldn't get through. It would have to wait.

He picked a few of the fruits and put them in his saddlebag. He would have them tested.

He headed back to Jaramillo Amba and chatted with some natives with fincas nearby. He asked about strange plants and mutations in their crops, but there was nothing abnormal in the area they knew about. It would be a localized lode if that was what it was.

He went to his car and paid for the use of the Palomino, which had been an excellent mount, well-trained and easy to get along with. He put the bag of fruit in the car and headed back to his own car. He was in David just a little after eight o'clock. He called Dave and got him this time. He asked about the strange apparent mutations he'd found. He had to tell Dave just what kinds of fruits and what the differences in the plants seemed to be.

"It's not radiation mutation. That would result in deformities in that much variety. It's something else.

"You said a chinaberry tree? I've never seen one here. *Melia azederach* "Indica"? Neem?"

"I don't know what the hell that is."

"Is it the same chinaberry we had in Florida?"

"I'd say so. It even smells like it."

"I see. Someone is doing some fancy ... it can't be hybridization. It would be something that's being done through genetic engineering today. They're designing those edibles with an added something. Possibly poisons of one kind or another. Be glad you didn't taste any of them!

"Have them tested ... I've heard a lot about *azederach* lately. Mostly neem oil. It has a lot of properties we use in agriculture. It has a lot of natural medical properties. Over a hundred odd chemicals that can be used in naturopathic cures and so forth.

"If there had been a *Prunus armeniaca* there I would say someone is trying to breed or engineer a definitive cancer cure. B seventeen isn't found in any of those things."

"What's a *Prunus armeniaca*. I didn't notice

everything there."

"Apricot. You would've noticed if there had been one. Have all those fruits tested to see if they have any of the compounds found in *azaderach* in them. I'd suggest you find someone who has the equipment who isn't someone another government can get to. This would have to be kept secret."

"Another government?"

"They were doing research to insert poisons in food crops back in the late seventies through the mid-eighties. The excuse was to find methods before the enemy found them so you could have an antidote for them handy. Most governments were working on that kind of thing. Typical military crap. I don't quite get it, because the poisons in *azederach* don't affect people to any extent. They can kill hogs and cows, but not people. This isn't with anything that would be fed to hogs or cows.

"When you find which chemicals are inserted you'll find the rest of it. It'll be obvious."

"I'd say it would have to be something that's cumulative or something. If the first person ate a banana and died, it wouldn't be an hour before the stuff was found."

"That's why it doesn't make any sense to me."

Clint took the fruits to a lab his friend, Manolo, who worked parttime undercover for Interpol et al recommended. He asked if they could find anything from list "A" – the chemicals found in *azederach* – in most or all of the fruits. They would have the results in forty eight hours.

He didn't know anything else to do. He went back to Bocas Town. He called Tyna, but her phone was turned off. He called Judi, but her phone was also off.

Had they gone to Quebrada Tula, where there was no signal?

At five o'clock sharp his throwaway phone buzzed. Only four people knew that number. Tyna was one of them. It was her. She had some things to tell him. "Clint this is the phone of a friend. I think someone can trace mine. I've turned it off. Judi turned hers off.

"We weren't here for two hours before some people came from Bocas and asked about us. Basilio said we'd talked about going to Quebrada Tula and had left the boat there. He checked the boat when they were in town. There's a small GPS marker or something in it. He'll take it out and throw it into the ocean if you wish. Judi says that means there's probably one in your car. Be careful.

"Judi checked over everything in her luggage. I did too, and Nito's things. She found one of the things. She has a little flashlight on her key chain. It didn't work. She knew it did last week. She opened it and found a little thing inside. We put it on the boat back to Chiriqui Grande. I found something like it in Nito's toys. It went on the boat, too. I think mine will be in my phone. I took the battery out."

"Leave it on the boat. You can leave it on the dock there if you go anywhere.

"Who came there?"

"Dr. Edna Markham and that LeSeur person."

They chatted awhile. Clint called Sergio, who said he would check out Markham thoroughly. Nothing else had happened.

Clint took the water taxi to Isla Colón, cleaned up, and went around town. He saw three of the doctors, who all asked where his wife was. He told them she went onto the comarca to get away from the harassment in Bocas Town. He ran into Blakely, who asked about Panamá City (Oh? He knew Clint was going to Panamá City?) He said he didn't go all the way because he found what he needed to know in David. He visited some friends while he waited for the information he'd requested.

He finally went home and to bed.

In the morning he met with Sergio. He told him about part of what he'd been doing. He'd gone to Jaramillo Amda, because that was fairly close to where Dave was shot at. There had to be a reason for that location.

"And did you find the reason?"

"Yes, but I'm waiting for some results to know the reason. It seems to be about unique plants, but not *Anthurium*.

"Sergio, we have to know everything we can learn about what Harry Fairbanks and Morris Goodman are up to. Who are they?"

"I can give you what I have. You're better at tracing people than we are." He found the file and gave it to Clint, who took it to his place to use his computer.

Goodman had several small businesses in the states, mainly Texas and Virginia.

Red flag!

Further back: he was born in Butte, Montana, in October of 1964, moved to Atlanta, Georgia, 1967, basic schooling in Atlanta until 1977, moved to Jacksonville, Florida, 1977. UF grad MS 1989, Moved to Houston, Texas, 1989 through present. Opened medical research clinic 1990 – present.

Opened (w/partnerships) natural medicine shops (3) 1996. Houston, Texas; Atlanta, Georgia; Richmond, Virginia. Traveled extensively. Social life, unknown,

What had happened between 1977 and 1989? Twelve years? He simply ends up a MS?

It had to do with plants. He was a botanist of one sort or another.

Clint went to UF records and checked out the old yearbooks 1985 – 1989. Morris William Goodman studied medicinal botany and was an exceptional student in genetics. He had proven better at some techniques than his professors.

Gee! That wasn't in his official history! Clint learned years ago that those old yearbooks are scanned and in the records on the websites of the school. Establishing a new "record" for any reason doesn't take those older books off the web. Once on the web, always on the web. They can change whatever parts they want, later, but someone, somewhere, will have the whole mess recorded and available. Clint wasn't about to reveal one website that stays accurate. The powers that be would find a way to "modify" it.

Okay. This confirmed in Clint's mind what he was beginning to suspect. He just couldn't figure why or how.

He studied organic poisons on various sites. He

figured what fruits were being used for instead of other crops. Heat broke a lot of the faster and more virulent types down. Whatever this was, it was in the uncooked fruit. That was why these were chosen.

Fairbanks' records were from 1990 to present and were totally blah. There was a notation at the beginning that said he was born in Elstonville, Wyoming, and spent his entire youth there. A fire destroyed the entire center of town, including the hospital and courthouse. It was a town of only two hundred people at the time. It was never re-established. Fairbanks was working for a trucking company in 1990 until he moved to Panamá. He is living in Panamá at present.

Gee! He worked for a trucking company for who knows how many years and didn't have a driver's license or tax records they could check?

Now Clinton Faraday had a damned good idea of who Goodman and Fairbanks were and a basic idea of what kind of thing they were doing. It still didn't make sense. Hits would be certain to cause some very close and dangerous, to them, investigation.

Wait a minute!

He called the secret number and soon had Judi on the line.

"Did Fairbanks ever mention having been anywhere in the states?"

"What kind of question is that? I only talked with him a couple of times. He did say he knew Tampa and Orlando when I said I came here from Florida."

"Thanks. That may be enough."

They chatted for a few minutes. Markham and LeSeur had left. Basilio made it plain to them that she and Tyna had come to the comarca to get away from their kind of people and they were *not* going to Quebrada Tula. If they pursued harassing his people more he would ban them from going to the comarca anywhere or at anytime. Dave had called and they told him about it. He would leave a hint that he was going to Soloy, which is in the comarca. Basilio sent word to Soloy that, should any gringos come there asking about Dave, they were to be escorted off the comarca.

Clint went to the police station. The research on Markham and LeSeur was in. LeSeur was hard to trace. Markham was what she seemed to be, but also had a somewhat shady period in her past. Clint checked his sources quickly and found she was almost an anarchist, claiming governments always acted against their people after a few years from when they were established.

Maybe that would fit!

"I checked Susan Blakely a little better, seeing she and Markham are both Australian. She was what she seemed, mostly. She was concerned about the environment and the ecological chains. She was against the ravages to the environment pollution and strip mining and so forth are doing.

"Clint, she, Markham, LeSeur, and Bianco are into international conspiracy theory, to an extent. Does this connect with that?"

Clint sat back with a sour grimace. "It could, Sergio. It very damned well could!

"Did the lab ... I have to check with them! It could give us our answers!" He went to the phone and asked if the tests were complete yet. Another three hours.

He thought. He went back to the computer. He couldn't find anything about Fairbanks.

Okay. Fairbanks was either witness protection, CIA, or some other covert organization.

He called Manny Mathews, who used to be Marko Boccini. He was one of the most powerful dons in the world. After a couple of minutes of chat, he asked about Fairbanks. He gave Manny what he had.

"Oh. Judy said he once mentioned being in Tampa and Orlando. That isn't in the records."

"Gimme half an hour. I'll call."

Clint and Sergio tried a few scenarios that didn't solve anything. Twenty four minutes later Manny called.

"'Irish O'Connor'. Detroit. Bernadetti group of

Greco's end of the Doniletti mob. I got along with Greco and Artie. Very pro hit. Ass in a crack and had to testify against a goat. Goat was more than a goat. He had to disappear. Set up to look like he was hit. One hit and ID'ed as him was a drug runner the 'F' got. He looked enough like Irish to pass, seeing his body was in a fire that messed his face up."

"So. He's working for CIA or military intel?"

"No. If he's into anything, it's unauthorized."

"Thanks, Manny. We're in a big mess and can't figure out who's behind it."

"I did a fast check when Dave got shot at. It wasn't very deep or I'd have taken care of Irish already. That's his MO. I'll bet Dave's the only hit by him that missed in twenty years. He got that Knight woman. Was that an alternative?"

"If Dave told her about what they're doing – which he only suspects – it could have been."

"That Goodman character is heavy into plant medicine. If they found a cancer cure or something, maybe they want to protect the hundred billion dollars they're going to make?"

"It could be, I guess, but it's no cure for anything they're after. At least, I don't think so."

They talked a few minutes, then Clint rang off. He and Sergio went to Don Chicho's for a snack, then back to get the lab results on the fruit. It came in fax. There were seven things found in all of them as well as in the *Melia azederach.*

It didn't mean anything to Clint. He didn't dare trust any of the botanists here who might know.

He called Dave. Dave said he had a list of things found in *Melia azederach* somewhere. Give him a minute to bring it up on the comp. It took six minutes, but he found it.

"Okay, give."

Clint gave the first one. "Very good against intestinal parasites. Great for treating *psoriasis.*"

The second. "Minor anti-inflamant."

The third. There was a pause, then, "Seems to be a very good lasting contraceptive." There was another pause. "This is something! It works as a contraceptive on both male and female. It causes sterility, but temporary."

"They might have found the pill for men?"

"That would be purely stupid. They have the *azederach* already. I wonder why nobody's ever tried extracting and marketing."

The fourth. "Another insecticide that affects mites as well as larger ... it's more a repellant."

The fifth. "Mild anti-irritant."

The sixth. "An absorbent."

"Which means?"

"It's like DMSO, but weaker. It makes things easy to absorb."

The seventh. "No application listed. Chemical structure might make it a reductor."

"Reductor?"

"Makes things dissolve slower. Sort of like putting the medicines in gelatin. Mixed. Not like a capsule."

"So. What does it cure, taken as a whole?"

The man at the desk called for Sergio. They had an incident. Sergio went out. Dave continued, "A couple are there because the insert carried them. They don't have any purpose. I can't think of anything it would cure internally that they don't have better already ... maybe one thing."

"One thing?"

"It cures babies."

"Cures babies of what?"

"No. Taken in very small doses, there won't be anymore babies. There wouldn't be side-effects or symptoms. This could be an answer to one of the biggest – actually, the biggest – problem of the world today. Painless, not debilitating."

"Population control?"

"Births as much as stop in a given group. No one gets sick. They even have a better general health. Not one is in pain more than usual. They simply stop having kids. The death rate remains the same. The number of people in that section decreases by the death rate. There is no birth rate. Forty years, the population is in balance with everything else. There won't be any births because the would-be mothers are past menopause."

"Then it would be a good thing?"

"Overall. There are a few problems that are huge!"

"Yeah. Which section do you use it on. *Not* on mine!"

"That, but more importantly, how do you not sterilize the ones with genetic qualities the race needs? How do you know you aren't sterilizing the would-be father or mother of the next major genius who can save the entire human race from something? It would have to be accomplished truly randomly. Any selection would necessarily not include me or my family or my business partners or politicians or priests and preachers or on and on. It could be a boon or a catastrophe, either big beyond description."

"So. If the conspiracy theorists are correct, it would accomplish pretty exactly what the ones suspected want?"

"Yeah."

"So you'd better start hitting any theorist who might get word out. Then why you? You aren't a conspiracy theorist."

"Because I would note the difference in the plants, as you said long ago. I would bring an investigation.

"I don't doubt there's a conspiracy. I just have the sense to know we're not going to be able to do anything about it. We can live with the Indios and avoid most of it. If they think they can use something like this on the Indios, they damned well don't know me ... which is why they would have to get rid of me."

"Maybe you have a way to thwart them they don't know about?"

"I hate the idea. Yeah. It would damned soon become survival of the fittest, but the fittest to a different kind of world."

"What can I do? There's a professional hit man near the head of this."

"Eliminate that one. Try to get it to where ... cripes! In this world, who can handle this?"

"We can destroy those plants and get rid of Goodman and Fairbanks."

"So? It's been done. Fifty other can do it in fifty different places. The results are fixed. It's now a matter of ten years or less."

"So all we can do is try to tell the world they're doomed?"

"And sound like the conspiracy theorists? The same ones would even hear you.

"Clint, we're not doomed. The ones who are doomed are the as yet unborn. They simply won't be born.

"Clint, what those idiots behind this aren't considering is that their children will end up in a world where the same things will happen on a smaller scale. What happens when the next one thinks your family should be out of the equation? What happens when your own progeny has the means and thinks some other family who pissed them off should go?

"It isn't a simple question. There's no simple answer. You're a private detective who brings killers to justice, such as exists. There is a killer here. He is also important to a project that he is the last kind who should have any say in, whatever.

"Do your part. I'll have to check some things out. There may be a way to dilute the effects of this and make it something they don't dare use. I have to have seeds and pollen from all of it. Can you get that without them knowing?"

"I can damned well try!"

They hung up after a few more words. Clint said to Sergio, "Arrest Fairbanks for murder. He's a known hit man living here under an alias. Dave was shot at and Susan Knight was killed by his MO. Goodman was seen driving him out to where Dave was shot at. He's accessory."

"It's that big?" Sergio asked.

"That's such a tiny part of how big it is you can't even see it.

"Sergio, Dave and I know what this is about. It's far better for everyone that we remain the only two who are sure."

"You were asking him about cures. What does this cure?"

"Babies."

Sergio gave him a funny look and shrugged. He called for the truck and four armed officers. They were going to arrest a professional killer. They were to take no chances.

They left. Clint sat there for a few minutes, then went home. He called Tyna and said she and Judi were to actually go to Tula. This might get very, very hairy!

The Final Puzzle Pieces

"He tried to stand us off. You said he had to be out of the equation. He shot Officer Cano. We shot him. I think he was hit more than a dozen times. Goodman was in the line of fire. Tough shit!" Sergio said. "Clint, Cano was a good man. We can't have this kind of thing here. We won't! If I have to accidently shoot every single one of those plant people, I'll do it! Personally!"

"I have to find which ones are into it. Some of them are here to stop it, some are here for the _Anthurium_ find, some are in it.

"The only one I don't have a real idea about is Blakely. He doesn't seem to fit, except as a greedy arrogant man who wants to steal the thunder for a plant discovery. The puzzle there is that he knew about it before the information could have gotten to him. That means someone here. It could mean Goodman or Fairbanks.

"I don't much like him, so I have to temper my reactions. I'm human. I may be subconsciously looking for a goat.

"Markham and LeSeur are a combination of two who are probably here because of the plant find and truly want to preserve the species while getting personal credit for the find. The puzzle there is that I can't seem to be able to put those two together.

"Bianco and Castro are innocent of anything. They aren't involved more than as scientifically interested. Castro wants to find the same thing in Brazil, if it's found there. Bianco is interested, scientifically. She wants to get rights to cultivate it commercially.

"Schone is a puzzle. He could be the same as Bianco. It doesn't quite fit."

"So. We can concentrate on Blakely, Schone, Markham and LeSeur. I've already done thorough checks on Markham and LeSeur to the extent that I can. Blakely, is an arrogant asshole. He may also be British Intelligence. We've both seen them use that technique. Make yourself just obnoxious enough that others will dismiss them as being too unprofessional to be suspects in anything.

"Like you, I can't figure Schone.

"I've had all of them observed when they're here. Blakely went to the garden club meeting. How did he even know about it?"

Clint thought. He called the secret number, chatted with Tyna a minute, then asked Judi, "Did you go to the last garden club meeting the day before you left here?"

"Yes. I see. Blakely seemed to know Henrietta

Jackson. She's from England. That's how he knew about the *Anthurium* before anyone else. He knows her."

"I have to know why he knows her. What did she know about the plant and Dave?"

"Nothing. I told her Dave had found a new species. She grows a lot of *Anthurium* species at her little place on Bastimentos. She knows Dave from when he gave talks at the meetings."

"Then he's probably not involved past personal greed."

"I think that's about it. There were never any slips or pauses in the wrong places or anything. Even Henrietta said he tends to be pompous and trying.

"That's right! She met him at a lecture at Kew a few years ago. She kept up a bit of contact with her e-mail. She told me about meeting a famous botanist there who was interested because she had such a good collection of *Anthurium* at her place. She didn't tell me the name at the time, but we can assume it was him."

"Thanks, Judi. That lets the obsequious jerk off the hook, damnit!"

She laughed and rang off.

"Blakely's out of it, apparently. We have the three. None of them may be involved. What's going on was the kind of thing that must be kept secret. I think this might be the kind of thing nobody else would be involved in. They wanted to control the world, in a sick way. They might even have believed they could engineer a new world altogether in a way that wouldn't involve wars or such.

"*Not* Fairbanks! Goodman might have been the kind who ... no. He took Fairbanks there to kill Dave. He was here when Fairbanks killed Knight.

"He might have believed the end would justify the means. I'll have to see if he was Zionist."

"He was, but not radical. The philosophy is still that the end justifies the means."

"Then that part of the puzzle is solved. It's a matter of whether one or all of those three are involved past personal greed or whatever."

"I may make a suggestion?"

"Of course!"

"Schone is sitting at the Grill right now."

Clint nodded and stood to stretch. "I think I could use a chicha. Want to come along?"

"No. He would talk to you. I'm the police."

Clint nodded again and went out to casually stroll to the Grill. He spotted Schone and went directly over to sit across from him. He ordered a pineapple/orange chicha and said, "I don't think we've formally met. I'm Clint Faraday.

"Dr. Schone, will you tell me what you're here for or am I going to have to dig it out?"

He grinned drily, and said, "I came to try to get my hands on a major discovery in the botanical field and ended up involved in a murder. I know nothing about it and regret deeply that I came here. Had I done proper research of your friend I would have known from his several works with *Orquidea* that I was wasting my time and funds. He will name the plant for an Indigeno friend and give me, as you say in the states, the finger."

"Correct?"

"Mostly. He wants to name it after my son.

"Come to think of it, my son's Indigeno!

"He may not name it at all. Only he knows where it is and he doesn't want a lot of crap that will end with it becoming extinct in its natural habitat."

"I will arrange registration for him. I will seek nothing more. He need but to bring a plant here. I will arrange that he registers it as a find that he didn't recognize at the time. The location will be Bocas del Toro, Isla Colón, Panamá, with the GPS numbers for this town. Any one of us could have suggested that from the first and none of this would have happened."

"It would have. The murder wasn't because of the plant. It was brought to a head by the plant because someone stupid thought Dave found something else. An illegal operation."

"That Fairbanks and the Goodman character?"

"Right. The murder's been solved as to who committed it. We have to know who else was involved. It wouldn't have happened if only that plant was involved."

"I noted that Blakely came before he possibly could have if someone hadn't informed him?"

"Someone did. A woman he corresponds with at the garden club here. He met her at Kew. She's from England and raises *Anthurium*."

He sighed. "I was sort of hoping he was in hot water. He's, excuse me, an ass!"

"We agree on another subject!"

Clint called Dave. Schone talked with him for a minute, wrote a few things on a notepad, then handed the phone back to Clint.

"Clint? Show him the plant on your deck. We can hope it has another bud by now. He'll register it in my name. See if there's a way he can get credit of some kind. He's the first one of that gaggle since Susan who was honest with me."

They chatted for a minute and Dave rang off. Schone reached into his case and brought out a computer, then put it back.

"As soon as we can arrange it I will have to photograph the plant and view it for the proper description. When will be convenient?"

"Now?"

He looked surprised. He called the girl over for

the cuenta. He and Clint got a taxi and went to Clint's place. Schone took a very good camera from his carrycase and took what seemed like a hundred pictures from all angles. There were three buds, one just opening. Schone very carefully teased it open enough to see the colors and form. They then went to Clint's computer where Schone contacted the university where he taught and had a form on the screen he filled out. It took an hour. Schone was agonizingly careful. When the form was done, Clint read it over and added a line on the discoverer's section.

Located and described by Dr. Gustav Arnold Schone, DrSc.

"That seems to about cover it," he said.

"Thank you, Clint. It seems my name will be connected with the major find of the century in *Anthurium* after all! All I ever had to do from the inception was be honest!"

"Dave's like that."

They went back to town. Schone would take the flight out in the morning to return to Germany.

"Another piece in place. Two to go," Clint told Sergio.

"We progress."

"Do you know where Markham and LeSeur are now?"

Sergio made a call. "Gualaca. They're going to

look in La Fortuna. Isn't that where it is?"

"No. Close. They may find one there, but it's registered. It will be for nothing.

"I'll happen to run into them there. Maybe I can learn a thing or two." He soon said his farewells and went home, then used Ben's boat to go to Almirante. Ben was a neighbor who sometimes used Clint's boat.

He arrived in Gualaca about three o'clock and found that Markham and LeSeur were taken to a spot in a taxi, which returned for them at six if they were in an area of no signal for the phones. The taxi driver said they were dropped between Smithsonian and the dam. About halfway.

He drove out. He spotted them coming out of a path to an electrical tower. He stopped and went to talk. LeSeur said they were going to look in all the places on government land until they found the plant. Clint said it was registered. He had a plant on his deck in Bocas Town, that Schone had done the description and recording, and that this was comarca, not government land.

"You have one of them all this time right there in Bocas Town!?" LeSeur cried. "It is registered?! *Schone*? Why?"

"Because he was honest with Dave. That was all Dave asked of anyone. It was named after my son with Dave the discoverer and Dr. Schone the one who located it on my deck. The location it was taken from was listed as unknown, but in either Chiriqui or Bocas del Toro Province."

His cel buzzed. It was Sergio.

"Clint? I just wanted to tell you that Dr. Schone suggested that we get what he calls a CITES certificate and make a law that the plant may not be legally moved after today's date anywhere in the country and only as seed that is proffered by Dave, personally, with a certificate stating the law and with his signature attached. I contacted the agricultural ministry. We have made the certificate application. The legislature is meeting at eight o'clock tonight to pass the law as stated by Dr. Schone.

"Dr. Schone has my respect. He's very damned careful about these things!"

"Thanks, Sergio. I'm with Dr. Markham and Dr. LeSeur right now. I'll tell them. Caio!"

"Tell us what?" Markham demanded.

"That there is now a CITES certification. That there is a law here that you move any plant of that species, even one meter, you go to jail for two years. If you take one out of the country the international CITES committee will see that you're brought here to face a five year sentence and that any and all plants are returned. Dave may personally give you seeds and a certificate that they are from him. You may take as many as twelve seeds (he was making a lot of it up, but it was what he expected would be passed) under his signature. I think he's made an agreement that Dr. Schone can take fifty seeds as reward for his help."

"He didn't say all that!" LeSeur cried.

"He said law thirty two of September sixth, two thousand ten applies. I know the law. I helped Dave draft it. It was mostly for orchid species, but wasn't exclusive to them."

"Coises! Foiled again!" LeSeur said. "I guess we deserve it.

"Can we catch a ride back to Gualaca? I'll be glad to get back to the island for three or four days, then back to Stockholm. I *have* gained experience in the field, which will serve me well. I can write that part up and publish."

"Fair enough! Climb in!"

"I'll fight this!" Markham snarled. "You won't get rid of me so easily!"

"Dr. Markham, you played the game and lost. You made your bet and you took your chances. Whatever," Clint said. "If you'd come here and been honest, it could be you with the name of locator. You didn't. It isn't."

"Edna, be a sport! He's right!" LeSeur said.

"The plant isn't all that's involved here!" she snapped. "Perhaps there are other things I find more important?"

"Fairbanks and Goodman are dead," Clint said. She staggered.

"Who are Fairbanks and Goodman?" LeSeur asked. "What have you kept from me? I always knew there was something!"

"She was involved with a project that could have been a good thing in the right hands, but is a horror in the hands of the people controlling it."

"It is needed!" she cried. "It is salvation for the world, for the human race! It is *not* in the hands of evil people!"

"O'Connor was a professional hit man," Clint argued. "How can you say he was the kind of person to have control in any project?"

"He was necessary."

"So. It's what we said about Goodman. He might have been honestly concerned about things, but believed the end justifies the means.

"It does – sometimes, but this is a thing you haven't thought out halfway. It would end up destroying the people it was designed to hand the world to. They would all be people like you. The end justifies the means. My family is so much better and smarter that the Jones. Why not?

"Meanwhile, the Jones are thinking exactly the same about your family. You'd have the means."

She didn't have an answer to that. She probably

hadn't ever thought about it.

They didn't talk on the way back to Gualaca. When they got out she said, "And the project?"

"What the Indios haven't already destroyed will be handled. There isn't much." He knew by her smirk that some of this was already out.

Well, it had to happen. He could hope.

He headed back to Bocas Town. The puzzle was complete, but a piece or two might be lost.

An Interim

"Well, it seems we have an interim. The seeds will produce plants like those in the comarca. I crossed them with normal varieties and only a fourth of them came through with all of it. Nature gets rid of a lot of the unneeded genetic material through the natural processes," Dave said, two months later. The whole group were lazing around on Clint's deck for a going away party of sorts. Clint and family were going to Quebrada Tula for three or four months.

"So. It'll breed out after awhile," Judi said. "What did you do with the plants they had?"

"They're still there. Silvio is council head there and will see no one disturbs anything. They'll solve a problem we have on the comarca. It'll be done with permission of the people who eat the fruits," Dave answered. "There are families who they know shouldn't breed. Genetic flaws that can only get worse. The ones who have it agree they shouldn't have children, but fall in love, and do. Now they can still fall in love and not have children. It won't be by any decree of the council. They're very practical people and have already discussed sterilization. Now they can simply use the fruit that won't negatively affect them like so many mechanical methods do and won't depend on anyone taking the pill at critical times when they can't afford them and have to fight the church to get them."

"Markham was watched very carefully. She was contacting two people regularly. One in Mexico and one in Colombia. They are both producers of fruits for commercial use. There is a chance they made tests of the fruits. They are growing a great many of the trees. One is associated with a processing plant that produces juice for market in all of Central America. We thought heat during the processing would destroy the chemicals. It doesn't completely. One plant is experimental and uses minimal radiation for sterility. It doesn't affect the chemicals.

"A large barrio in Mexico City suddenly had its birth rate decrease by sixty eight plus percent. It stayed that low for more than three months, then returned to normal. Tests show the chemical can cause contraception for three months. We would estimate that sixty to seventy percent of the people in that barrio consume the juice from that plant. A side effect we didn't consider was that the general health was better for that time and a little more. Those compounds can be and are an aid when certain problems arise.

"It would work, Clint. The government has seized the places where the fruits are grown, but they haven't done anything to get rid of them. The heads of the government there are probably deciding which ten barrios get the next tests."

"There's no question of its working," Dave argued. "It's strictly a moral issue. We can't allow it to be in the hands of immoral people. At the same time there's no way we can stop it from eventually falling into the hands of the worst and least moral people on the planet.

"You have to realize that there are a lot of plans to kill off a large part of the population by far worse means. They're also less discerning means. A-bombs don't select their victims."

"And that's where the whole problem lies that we can't hope to solve," Tyna said. "Who gets to choose who it's used on?

"Finish the guanabana chicha. It won't keep."

C. D. Moulton's works are available on most major outlets as printed or e-books. CD writes the CD Grimes, PI, mysteries, the Det. Lt. Nick Storie mysteries, the Clint Faraday mysteries, the Flight of the Maita science fiction series, books on orchid culture and many others of many types. Mystery, adventure, intrigue, science fiction, humor, fantasy, paranormal, mild erotica, and factual.

www.ingramcontent.com/pod-product-compliance
Lightning Source LLC
Chambersburg PA
CBHW072205150726
48002CB00014B/1272